ABOUT YOU

AMIE TEMPLETON

LitPrime Solutions
21250 Hawthorne Blvd
Suite 500, Torrance, CA 90503
www.litprime.com
Phone: 1 (209) 788-3500

Published by LitPrime Solutions   11/06/2020

ISBN: 978-1-953397-31-7(sc)
ISBN: 978-1-953397-32-4(e)

CONTENTS

INTRODUCTION

T hose who have read my first book, This Song's For You, will know of the experiences I encountered following the death of my youngest son, and that for some years I feared for my sanity. I investigated the learning opportunities that came my way, yet the numerous courses I attended on my chosen subjects left me knowing there was much more to be discovered, although the goal was not yet clear. It took several more years of searching on my own before the fog started to lift and I began viewing the world through different eyes. With each moment of enlightenment, a bigger picture was gradually revealed, and it is becoming clearer as I continue my search. Much of the information in this book is by no means new. It has been written in many languages and forms over the years, and is there for the seeker to find.

We all have the same potential for spiritual growth, which leads to a clearer understanding of ourselves and others as human beings. Just how long it takes for these changes in us to come about can depend on how enthusiastically we pursue our goal.

1

W hen I was a child, I attended a Protestant Sunday school for a short time, but I could not understand why a part of its teaching was that a God I could not see, and who I thought did not know me, would be so eager to punish me. I queried this aspect one Sunday, but the teachers only scowled silently down at me from the distance of their seemingly great height.

Unsurprisingly it was not long before my attendance at Sunday school petered out, but not before leaving me with lingering thoughts that we have a soul. It is generally believed that we are three-part beings of Body, Mind, and Soul. We can see our body; we interact with our mind, yet the soul seems to be ever-elusive.

I had read of a doctor who said he had opened up many, many people – both living and deceased – but had never once found a soul. I have learnt that because something cannot be seen does not mean that it does not exist.

2

I n the past, people who had knowledge of "The Secrets of the Universe" kept it to themselves because they thought that it would be dangerous in the hands of the general population, who they said were 'unprepared to hear it.' Also, people who spoke earlier languages, and who understood pieces of the ancient truths, were either unable or reluctant to explain them to others in simple terms. A study of the Ancient Egyptians, The Aztec Civilisation, or the Hindu religion can be enlightening.

Why are some people 'unprepared to hear?' Mostly it can be blamed on early conditioning. The young and vulnerable, are taught certain crucial 'facts' of how life works and what to expect from it. They learn that if they go to school and get a good education they might have an opportunity to further their education at college or university. Then they might enter a fine profession of their choice, get married, have a family, and live happily from that day forward. For those unable to go to college or university, their usual path could be to find a job after a few years of high school, and later to be married with one or two children. Such destinies have seemed logical enough to young minds, and so most have followed along with it.

Many are ignorant of the fact that in this way they are, in a sense, anchored to the Earth, and so it becomes natural to concentrate on the physical side of their lives. They do not know that it is possible to expand their consciousness, and consequently they reach adulthood with no reason to question why they are here, or what life is all about. People need to understand themselves if they are to live as the spiritual beings that we all are - each of us possessing that little bit of the greater subconscious - and to openly pass on this knowledge for the benefit of future humanity.

The goal of self-realisation can take time. First, we need to understand what this means, and then we need to do what is necessary to achieve it. Most of us must persevere if we are to become aware of who we truly are. We need to believe, or at least *begin* to believe, in the possibility that the soul exists. The next step is to seek it out.

By withdrawing our attention from the world around us, it becomes possible to discover that the answers all lie within us. We only need to learn how to access them.

3

The ability to reach beyond our five senses is not limited to just a chosen few. Everyone has the potential to develop self-awareness - it does not have boundaries - yet most people unknowingly travel the more difficult road. Sometimes a point is reached in their lives where they become aware of a far more wonderful pathway that is begging for their attention.

Some people might pretend ignorance because of a desire to fit in with the crowd. Others are content with their lives, believing nothing could bring improvement, especially if it might lead them somewhere beyond their imagination. Some have spent so long blocking their own power that they easily accept that "this is all there is."

Within all of us there is a divine spark of something far grander, yet while we are in human bodies we will surely make a few misjudgements in our lives. We cause our own suffering by believing we'll go to hell in a hand-basket if we dare to, for instance, abandon our religion, or even steal an apple if we are nearing starvation. On the other hand, we will suffer in some way if we choose to taste a little of what is morally wrong, and fear of consequences generally prevents us from making the same mistake twice.

4

Awakening can begin from an experience as simple as watching birds in a tree and wondering how they know how to fly or build a nest, or where to find food to feed their babies. Or it could happen after watching autumn leaves fall, then later seeing new growth sprouting and questioning how these wonderful events could occur. This does not necessarily apply to everyone because some people, from a young age, understand that the road to finding themselves is the most natural direction to follow.

Often, our inward search can be triggered by trauma, such as the loss of a loved one. It can begin at a time when we are at rock bottom; when everything that was considered of value is lost. At such times we plead for answers to the questions: "What is this life all about? What is there now to live for?"

Some people accumulate wealth, live in beautiful homes, and have absolutely all they could wish for. They might begin one day to receive such thoughts as "I have all I could possibly achieve. What else is there to life? How come we live merely to die? There must surely be something more!"

Any of these thoughts can be a major turning point,

and once we commence "soul searching," much of our former life is left behind. At first the changes might be very subtle, and not be recognised immediately. At a deeper level our thought patterns alter permanently and we begin to see things differently.

That which constitutes a disaster for one person could be flicked away like a speck of dust by another. This means that if we were to use a scale of one to ten, the event of, say, losing all your possessions in a house fire could be a 'three' for one person, yet a 'ten' for another. If we could then monitor the high number of those who have experienced the beginnings of awareness following a negative event, we would see that there exists an intelligence that knows what it is doing when delivering the various incidents.

Why do we rarely look deeper into ourselves until a crisis occurs? The answer is that up to that point we think we are controlling our own lives. Then the loss, misfortune or other trigger arises, and we find we are floundering with no signposts - no direction.

At such times the soul sits on the edge of its seat in expectation as it were, waiting to be acknowledged, and waiting for us to reach out for help and to ask "What do I do next?" At first we ignore this inner nudging, thinking we can fix things by ourselves. We make plans, but never seem get to where we think we should be going.

Our world is a magnificent place, where flowers and trees and fields of grain appear to grow of their own accord. What tremendous magic this is! How can we not wonder if we are more than physical beings when such miracles surround us every minute of our lives?

5

If we are guided only by our personal experiences, even beginning our inner search can be extremely challenging, particularly if using only those personal experiences to show us the way. It does not help when we do not know where we are heading, and for this reason many of us have travelled the long way around. As harsh as it might sound, feelings of discontent with our lives are self-inflicted, because they are brought about by thoughts of our own imagined imperfection. Each of us has the ability to achieve anything we wish, and yet when we try to picture the future success of a dream we create hurdles for ourselves. *"It won't work, it will take too long,"* or *"I can't see myself taking care of all those details."* And the list of reasons *not* to pursue our goal goes on.

If we refuse to accept thoughts of our perceived physical or mental inadequacies, the pure light of our soul can shine through.

6

You might have a problem that seems to be unsolvable, and you have nowhere to turn. If so, stop thinking about your dilemma for a moment; relax and quieten your mind. Close your eyes, pull any thoughts that you have sent out there back into yourself, and shut off the outside distractions. Then picture a Genie standing in front of you. This Genie can represent the greater subconscious, and will deliver to you anything you desire. He is waiting for you to tell him how he can help you.

From your place of centredness, use your thoughts, or you can speak aloud, to explain your situation. Then ask him for an answer to your problem. Be concise, yet specific, otherwise the Genie will not receive the true meaning of your request. Rehearsing your words beforehand can be helpful.

The energy of a thought cannot normally be seen, but nor can the energy of a magnet. This does not mean the energy does not exist.

You could say, "Genie, I would love a new house." You could add a description of the plan of your preferred house, and whether you would like four or maybe five bedrooms, and so on.

See yourself living in your chosen house with a new car in the garage – and having a well-paid job of your choice.

Remember to bring your feelings into it and feel grateful, as though what you are asking for has already been received. Then don't doubt for a minute that the Genie will bring you what you have wished for. Nothing is too much to ask of him. There is always enough. The supply never runs out. It is no use having a yearning and then turning the object of your desire upside down by thinking it will never happen. You need to convince yourself that your goal has already arrived. This can be accomplished by visualising and feeling the changes you will experience when your objective has been achieved.

It is essential to remember that when the request has been made or the problem handed over, it must be let go. There is never any need to stress, lose sleep, or worry over a situation that seems insurmountable. Allow your Genie - the energy of the Universe – to do the work for you.

A fleeting wish or a hope will not do it. Those methods will no doubt work further along humanity's road, when we have learnt to control our thoughts completely. At this stage of our evolution, and until we trust unconditionally in what we are doing, our message must be regularly defined,

When we have attuned to these natural laws and have come to where we accept that there is enough of everything for everybody, manifesting our desires will come more easily.

7

When we understand that the answers lie within the subconscious, we begin to recognise changes in ourselves. One of the best-known ways to begin making contact with the subconscious is through meditation. There is a peace that exists in the great depth of the sea, and we can discover that same peace by shifting our focus from daily activities and taking our consciousness to the quiet place that is within each of us.

Meditation does not take us outside of ourselves to the 'vast unknown', where, as is sometimes suggested, we might suffer all manner of negative experiences. It takes us safely inside ourselves to a realm of peace and tranquillity. When the active mind is shut down temporarily and we find we are in the presence of this sea of peace, our consciousness can start to expand. This is when awareness of ourselves is able to come to the fore – either in tiny increments, or at times as a sudden awakening.

This introspection is the answer to slowing our constant stream of thoughts. This is how we can move towards self-discovery; to forget almost everything we have been taught about how things work in several areas of our lives. Those well-trodden paths will not take us to where we need to go.

When just one foot has been placed on this path the understanding comes to us that the only way to move is forward. A new state of existence can actually be felt when the expansion of the mind has begun. Our thinking changes and we feel different. We wonder how we had previously been able to find our way through what now seems like a fog that relentlessly surrounded us.

Our soul continues to recognise what is happening and thereafter constantly urges us to seek something more - something much better. Yet it can take some time for that same recognition to filter through from the subliminal level to our conscious level.

After several meditations all might still appear the same as before when we return to our immediate surroundings, as though nothing has changed. Yet all the while there is unseen movement within us. We could say it was more of an emotion that we cannot quite identify.

If we regularly put aside some time to go to this place of peace, even for a few minutes, the results will soon become more apparent. Maybe it will seem that the world is changing, although it is ourselves who are doing the changing and we are seeing that same world differently.

8

Those who have begun their search seem to know instinctively that there is much yet to be discovered and understood and to be fused with the parts of the picture already in place in their minds. Even though the 'picture' could come in actual pictures, the information is more likely to come in the form of feelings, or simply as a 'knowing,' rather than visually.

As with anything that is meaningful, there are no "quick fixes". Self-discovery can take any number of years, but when we notice that changes are taking place in our consciousness, we find we can never give up our search, and neither can we unlearn what we have learnt.

We are unable to fully comprehend anything unless we have experienced it, because then we will always know how it feels. Simply having it explained is not enough.

Take for instance losing sight of your toddler on a crowded beach for 30 seconds before finding the child again. Those long 30 seconds will have given you a frightening insight into the emotions attached to the experience, and you will remember how this felt for the rest of your life.

Spiritual experiences leave us with that same memory and emotions. They become part of us, and change us from the person we once were.

Perhaps you know what it is like to temporarily leave your body, as in Astral Travel, or you might have had a near death experience. Others could be of the opinion that these happenings were in your imagination, and because of this, initially you might possibly doubt yourself, but when you re-think what happened, you will realise the Truth of the matter. Those accompanying feelings and memories do not go away. If you were not already on a spiritual path, you would no doubt set off on one, and that search would continue throughout your lifetime. Little by little we change from the person we were to the person we are becoming. It is only as time passes and we look back at our previous self that we are able to distinguish the difference.

9

As our thoughts and feelings become different as well as deeper, they create changes in our mind, and can cause us to become quieter in our daily lives. It is not unusual at this stage for a friend, acquaintance or relative, to remark that they are concerned for our mental stability. One or two could fade from our lives and they might spend a long time feeling sorry for us, while we continue our search for the keys that unlock the secrets of life.

If someone we might consider confiding in is not pursuing the same goal, it is better to keep to ourselves because our words would most likely fall on deaf ears. It is wise, therefore, to "Keep the butterflies under your hat" as author Stuart Wilde used to say.

When someone asks, "How does this work?" that person will be ready not only to hear but to understand your explanation. And even then, it is prudent to give answers in simple terms and not to elaborate. In some cases, your answer to their first question might lead them to ask more questions. This is when you will know they are receptive.

10

When we say, "It didn't occur to me," we mean the thought didn't come to us. All that has been created, and every situation that has ever transpired has become a reality as a result of a thought in someone's mind - from walking to the front gate and checking the mailbox, to the most ingenious of inventions.

In both examples above the thoughts are positive, yet we are all aware that thoughts can also be negative. For example, an elderly person is knocked to the ground and injured on the street and their belongings are stolen, or someone is murdered. Neither of these events can take place unless the thought of carrying them out enters the mind of the person responsible. People always have the option of discarding their unlawful thoughts, but for those who have taken on the role of villains in this lifetime, the desire to act upon such thoughts seems right at the time.

It would be rare for any person never to have received negative thoughts. But the thoughts themselves do not cause good or bad things to happen. They happen because the thoughts have been accepted and then put into action.

It is fortunate that people such as inventive technicians and builders carry through with information they receive in their thoughts, even though they might have reason to cast aside their ideas as being impractical or unachievable.

11

In order to contribute to a change of destiny, thoughts themselves need not always be negative.

For example, picture a man called Martin as he jumps into his vehicle and heads off through the traffic on his way to work. A minute or two later he finds himself thinking about his friend John.

"Wonder what he's doing later today? Maybe we could catch up for a beer."

During the day he calls John, and they agree to meet that afternoon.

John is already there when Martin walks into the tavern. "Hi mate," says John. "How're you doing? Long-time no see! "

Martin says, "Yes, it's been a couple of months. Far too long. How's Meagan and the kids?"

After two or three light beers and some good conversation they both go their separate ways.

The next day Martin hears that John did not make it home. He was run off the road and killed by another motorist who had been speeding. Martin is grief-stricken and deeply regrets having contacted John to meet up. He blames himself for John's death.

Behind the scenes, John's allotted time on Earth was coming to an end and it was time for Martin to begin his spiritual search. The speeding driver was already somewhere in the wings. And so, the thought was given to Martin to contact John. Had he not made the decision to do so, John would still have died, but from a different cause, and Martin would still have been guided towards the beginning of his search.

12

Countless thoughts run through our minds daily, and while we might believe that we are creating those thoughts ourselves, the reality is that we are, in a sense, watching them come into our mind from the greater subconscious. It is at this stage of receiving thoughts that we have the capacity to decide which ones to act upon and which ones to reject.

We can train ourselves to deny certain thoughts, just as we have the choice to walk away from a person who is trying to sell us an item we do not wish to buy. We come to be who we are through our life-long selection of accumulated thoughts, impressions and feelings associated with the world we live in. We can become happy or depressed, generous or miserly, kind or cruel.

In this manner we design our own lives, since we are each the product of the thoughts we have accepted, and which define who we think we are. The result of these thoughts emerges as our ego and refers to the part of the personality we identify as 'me' or 'I' while in a physical body. Fear of death is created by the ego, and does not come from the part of us that is our eternal self.

One of our aims in life is to bypass the ego and discover the real self while we are still in the physical body, instead of at the point of physical death. We can begin to understand how this works when we are able to see ourselves as more than a physical body - more than a human being. When this point has been reached, we find that we will be further aware of the changes that are emerging in our perception of the world around us.

There might be times when we become aware of the need for forgiving along the way. This happens as a natural result of our new perspective as our own thoughts change, and we begin to understand that there is light in everyone. It is not just in this person and that person but not in the next.

13

The word 'God' can be used in reference to the Universe and all it contains. God is everywhere at all times. God is the space between, as well as within, all things. Anything we might class as non-living – a mountain or a lump of gold – is made of the same stuff as our bodies. The difference is in the rate of vibration. Our entire Universe is made up of atoms that are constantly in motion, and their speed determines whether they are liquid, gas, or solid.

Many of us have believed that this God energy was outside of us somewhere – untouchable and unfathomable – while it not only surrounds us but is us. God is not 'out there somewhere', but *is* in us all, and we are all connected. Each one of us is a part of 'It', and that same 'It' – or 'God' – also surrounds us in different stages of consciousness, or expression, of all that exists. Since the parts are connected, vibrations from one of them can sometimes be sensed in others. This is how a person who is genuinely psychic can deliver information to a living person from their deceased loved one. Psychics have the ability to connect to those energies that are beyond the normal range of our senses.

There have been various accounts of a smoke-like form leaving the body at the point of death. Similarly, there are countless reports of people who have seen visions of loved ones who have departed from this Earth. Some incredible stories have been documented in these areas, so I will not elaborate here. Details can easily be found in the many specialist bookshops that exist today.

The majority of people who have personally experienced similar events are led to the conclusion that we do not die as that word is usually understood. Until we are able to recognise the reality of who we are while in a physical body, this world will present us with numerous challenges, and we will ask ourselves why these painful experiences continue to appear in our pathway.

14

Human potential can be compared to the power that illuminates light globes. Imagine, for example, that globes represent the bodies of human beings.

The power that is available from all power sockets in, say, a ten-storey building, can be likened to life energy or the God Force itself. Every light globe in the building is connected to the same power source, and yet a globe here and there would no doubt be brighter than others. This can be explained by their different wattage.

In our example we can pretend that they all have the same wattage, and that each globe has a dimmer switch to raise or lower its illumination. The brightness of each globe will depend, of course, on where its dimmer switch is set. Similarly, each living thing is what it is because of the level of its dimmer switch, which is set in accordance with the level of higher consciousness that has been achieved.

As with the illustration of the ten-storey building, there is a power that is present everywhere at the same time here on Earth, and which is sometimes referred to as the God Force.

Picture the God Force as a huge mass of energy, and from this energy is a cord running to each person, plant, animal, or insect. Through all of these cords runs the power of the Universal Subconscious Mind – or that which we call God.

We all stem from the one source, and it is because of this connection to the God Force or Universal Mind, that as we begin our inward search our personal dimmer switch starts to rise, and continues to rise with every new level of our awakening.

As our consciousness - or awareness - continues to grow, we yearn for more knowledge and information, and recognition of who we are. This yearning is fed back to the Universal Mind. If the longing is strong enough, the Universal Mind brings the object of that longing into existence.

By continuing our search for answers, we will eventually become aware of the truth that we are a soul that needs a body to function on this Earth plane.

15

You are having a human experience. We are all having a human experience and we are all made of the same Stuff of the Universe. We are human as well as a part of God. Universal Energy – or God - is yourself – is us. This is who looks out through your eyes and the eyes of everyone around you.

When the time comes for us to leave this world at the end of every physical embodiment, we leave behind our accumulated ideas of self-ness, or the ego, consisting of our name, personality and beliefs. We are no longer the individual, or 'I', that we have come to know while confined to the body, and the part of us that is immortal, our soul, returns to the ocean of the subconscious.

We know that when a drop of water is added to a bucket of water, that drop can never again be identified or retrieved. Likewise, our soul – the piece of the subconscious that has been with us throughout our lifetime - mixes once more with the greater subconscious. If we were to fill a cup by dipping it into that ocean of the subconscious, we could view the cup as a physical body and the contents as a soul. And so it is that when we are re-born, a small amount of that ocean is either within, or is in close proximity to, our new physical body. If we then replace our image of the ocean with an image of all that exists, we would come to the conclusion that our soul – the part that animates us – contains a part of all that now exists or has ever existed.

We each have our own direct line to the same greater subconscious mind. That line might be temporarily blocked through lack of use, but by using mindful effort we have the ability to open the way for a clear connection. Meditation is the key to uncovering the power that is already inside us and the truth of who we really are.

16

There are various types of meditation, and our choice depends entirely on personal preference. Daydreaming in the sun might be the simplest form, and there is also meditation music, guided meditation, and different types of yoga. To varying degrees these practices help day-to-day thoughts drift away, to be replaced by insights, thus allowing us to gradually see the bigger picture.

An easy meditation to begin with could be something like the following example. You might like to record it so it can be listened to. First be sure you are in a relaxed position – either sitting in a comfortable chair or lying down, and with your eyes closed.

> You are walking along a pathway beside a river on a sunny afternoon. The water in the river is moving slowly along. Just like you, it is not in a hurry to go anywhere. A bird flies into view, and noiselessly lands on the water, then seems very much at home as he drifts along with the flow. You stand still and watch until he becomes a tiny speck

in the distance, then you continue on your way.

Soon you come to a bend in the river, and your path is taking you away from the water's edge. You can just see the water sparkling now and then through the trees. You are feeling very contented as you breathe in the fresh air and take in your surroundings.

Ahead of you, through the trees, you can see the shape of some kind of building, although you cannot make out any details from this distance. As you get closer, you can see that the building is a house, and it has a dark red tin roof and white walls. There is a well-kept front garden, and surrounding the house and land is an ageing, grey picket fence, held together with thick wire.

When you get even closer you can see a woman working in the front garden. She seems to be pruning the hedge, and gives you a wave with her gloved hand as you pass by her front gate, and you wave back to her.

As you walk further along, your

path brings you again near the water, and now the river has become a lot wider. Near the bank on the other side you can see some children splashing about, and can hear their laughter. You stop walking and take in this pleasant scene, before slowly heading back the way you have come. You pass the house with the dark red roof. The woman is nowhere in sight this time. You wonder whether she lives alone or has a family.

Now you see that your path is taking you once again nearer to the water. The sun is still shining but is beginning to set behind you.

Soon you find yourself back where you started.

When you feel ready, open your eyes, and slowly move your arms and legs to help bring yourself back to the present moment. Sit quietly for a few more minutes and think about how you felt during this meditation time, and whether you feel any different now. For example you might have experienced peace, and this feeling might have come back with you. Or perhaps you received thoughts that are different to your usual style of thinking. A great idea might have come to you, and you can't wait to start making this idea a reality. At first you might not experience anything at all except relaxation, and this is quite normal. But this will change if you continue to take yourself away from normal daily activities and enter your place of peace.

If we have never meditated, we cannot know the changes that it can bring within us. These changes are not always immediate, although they could sometimes occur during meditation. For instance, you might become slowly aware of a small change in your outlook, say, of the way you now view certain characteristics that you once felt were annoying in other people. You could find that now you see people in a different light, and maybe you have a better understanding of human nature in general. Once these changes become a part of us, from that point forward we can never be the same.

Meditation can help us to feel calm, or to cope with

a crisis, but it is also a spiritual practice. The biggest hurdle is our mind, and once we begin to show it who is the boss, so to speak, the rest is easy.

17

Although the choice is entirely up to our personal preferences, meditating on the Pineal Gland might be considered the most direct and time-saving course to take.

The Pineal Gland – or Third Eye – can be found by imagining one point just above the nose between the eyes, and another point in the centre of the crown of the head. The Third Eye is situated where these two places would meet inside the head and can be activated by concentration on that area.

If you are doing this meditation for the first time, keep in mind that the Third Eye can calcify if not exercised on a regular basis, therefore decalcification could take several meditations before you feel or otherwise notice any difference in yourself.

Close your eyes, then relax completely, and keep your mind on your slow, gentle breathing for twelve breaths or so.

Thoughts will continue to come to you at first. They will soon fade away as you remain focussed on your breathing. When you are feeling completely relaxed – look upwards, towards your third eye.

You could initially aim at holding your

concentration for about fifteen seconds. It might help to count the seconds in your mind as they go by. Next time you could extend the time to half a minute. Then one minute. Then several minutes at a time.

During the process, it is not unusual to feel a tingling sensation at the crown of the head and/or between the eyes. If this occurs, try not to be distracted, and look on it as progress being made.

18

We are not alone. The answers will come; they are there for us whenever we make the call - not always immediately, and not always as words. This energy - this power – is available for us to contact at any time.

ASKING QUESTIONS

Making contact with the greater Subconscious or Universal Mind.

Have your questions ready by writing them down. Keep them simple or the responses you receive might not be at all helpful.

For this exercise you might like to either sit at your computer, or sit at a table with a pen and pad ready to make any notes.

Concentrate on your breathing. Watch your breath as it enters and leaves your nostrils.

Take your time.

Relax completely before asking your questions.

A reply could come in the form of what could be taken as thoughts in your mind. It is possible that you might also see pictures. Stay relaxed, and focus on what you are receiving. Either write the words or write descriptions of what you are seeing, and when it feels as though the communication has ended, study what you have written.

Do not be disheartened if you receive no response, or the information you receive on your first attempt does not make much sense. If you are neither satisfied nor happy with what you have received, try again at another time, keeping in mind that your communication will strengthen with practice.

CONTACTING YOUR GUIDE OR HIGHER SELF

Close your eyes, and try to imagine what your Guide or Higher Self might look like. Try to picture him or her standing in front of you.

Take your time.

A name might come to your mind, or, through your closed eyes, you could see this name in writing. If you happen to open your eyes, do not expect to see a solid person, although you could see a shape or outline.

You could see in your mind the energy of someone who represents Love. Or you might see something that is symbolic to you.

Even if you receive no image, when you are ready, ask your question if you have one, or give an outline of your needs. Your words can be either in your mind or you can speak aloud.

Having done this, listen patiently with your mind for a reply.

When you feel that there is no further message

to come, slowly bring yourself out of the meditation and back to your surroundings. Then think about what you have received. Was the information helpful to you? Could you draw a picture of the person you were shown?

Again, if there should be no communication, or you are not satisfied with the information, try again at a later time. As with the first exercise, your connection will strengthen with practice.

Following are words taken from from a wonderful poem written by Mary Elizabeth Frye. This poem can be freely accessed from the Internet.

Do not stand at my grave and weep
I am not there. I do not sleep.
I am the sunlight on ripened grain
I am the gentle autumn rain
Do not stand at my grave and cry
I am not there. I did not die.

www.ingramcontent.com/pod-product-compliance
Lightning Source LLC
Chambersburg PA
CBHW031632200726
48288CB00019B/1397